JOHN HENRY
THE STEEL-DRIVING MAN

Retold by
VIRGINIA SCHOMP

Illustrated by
JESS YEOMANS

Cavendish
Square

New York

IT WAS THE LATE 1800s. AMERICANS WERE scrambling to crisscross the country with railroad tracks. The railroads would carry goods and people. They would open up coal and timber lands. They would help the country grow.

Building the railroads was hard work. The men of the work gangs hauled rock and shoveled dirt. They laid wooden beams and heavy steel rails. They blasted their way through tall mountains.

Listen! One man is singing. Soon all the workers join in. The picks and hammers rise and fall to the rhythm of their work song. The words tell a story of joy and pain, strength and pride and courage. They tell the tale of John Henry.

3

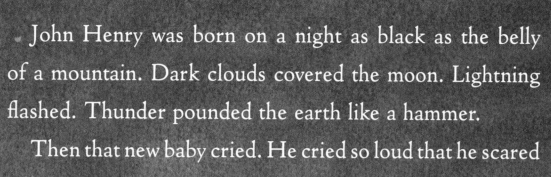

John Henry was born on a night as black as the belly of a mountain. Dark clouds covered the moon. Lightning flashed. Thunder pounded the earth like a hammer.

Then that new baby cried. He cried so loud that he scared off the storm clouds. A big copper moon gazed down from the sky. Crickets sang in the grass. Roosters crowed in the barnyard. Black bears roared and panthers growled in the woods and mountains. It seemed like the whole wide world was trying to say, "Welcome, John Henry!"

Folks knew right away that John Henry was something special. No one had ever seen a newborn baby walking and talking. And was that child hungry! When he was just one hour old, he asked his mama for supper. He ate four ham bones, a pot of greens, and a pan full of corn bread. He washed it all down with a bucket of buttermilk.

After his meal, the boy climbed up on his daddy's knee. He grabbed hold of a steel nail and his daddy's hammer. "I'm going to be a steel-driving man!" said John Henry.

Before long, John Henry was working on the plantation. He worked with the hoe. He worked with the ax, pick, and shovel. But the only tool that ever felt just right in his hands was the hammer.

As a young boy, John Henry hammered nails into boards. When he got older, he hammered fence posts. *Whoosh!* His big hammer swung through the air. *Whack!* The post sank into the hard ground like an ear of corn dipped in soft butter. As he worked, he sang in his powerful voice:

Born with a hammer in my hand.
Going to be a steel-driving man.

9

At last, the Civil War came and put an end to slavery. John Henry was a grown man. A *free* man. It was time to leave home and make his way in the world.

John Henry rambled all over the South, working at all kinds of jobs. He picked corn and cotton. He built roads and houses. He loaded cargo onto the steamboats that chugged up and down the Mississippi River. When each job was done, he moved on. He walked down the road, singing:

Gotta find me a job
With a hammer in my hand.
Going to be a steel-driving man.

After a whole lot of wandering, John Henry found himself in West Virginia. He hiked through mile after mile of tall, proud forests. He climbed up hills and down into hollows.

One day, a sweet sound rang out over the next hill. He scrambled to the top and peered down into a valley. He saw hundreds of workmen. He saw a road of shining steel rails. The men were building a new line for the Chesapeake and Ohio Railroad. And the beautiful sound that John Henry had heard was the *clang, clang, clang* of their hammers.

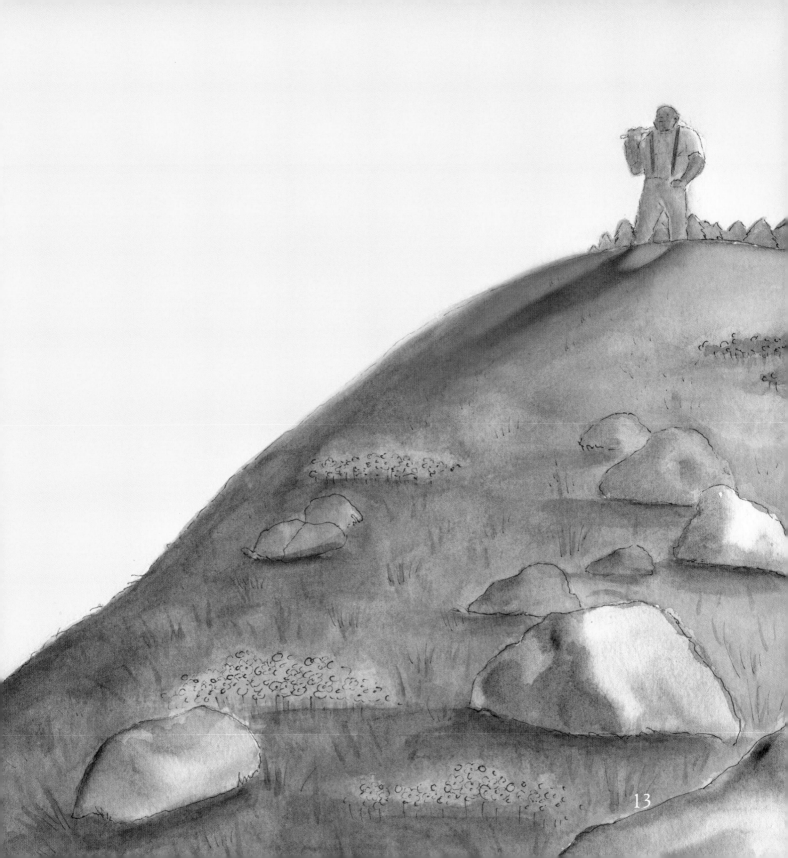

John Henry watched the workers closely. Some of them were laying wooden railroad ties on the ground. Others crossed the ties with heavy steel rails. Still others hammered in the spikes that would hold the rails to the railroad ties.

The hardest job of all was steel driving. The steel drivers had to drill holes into solid rock. A helper called a shaker held the steel drill in place. The steel driver pounded the drill with his heavy hammer. After he made a lot of holes, the blasting crew packed them with dynamite. *KaBOOM!* The blast blew the rock to kingdom come, clearing the way for more railroad tracks.

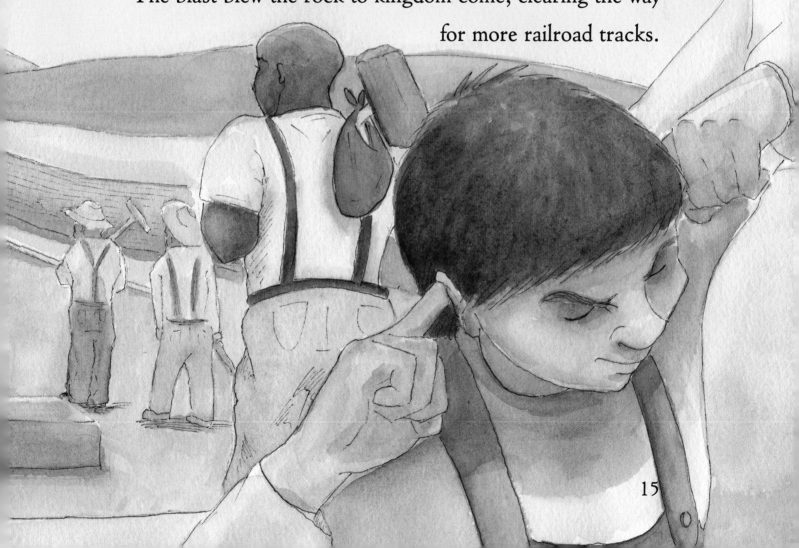

16

John Henry went to the captain of the railroad gang. "I was born to be a steel-driving man!" he sang out.

"Steel driving is hard work," said the captain. "You have to hammer fast, or you can slow down the rest of the gang. You have to hammer true, or you could hurt your shaker."

"Just give me a chance," said John Henry. Then he lifted his hammer. It flashed through the air like lightning. He brought it down with a crash as loud as thunder. With just one stroke, he drove his drill deep into the rock.

And the captain said, "You're hired!"

So John Henry set to work for the Chesapeake and Ohio Railroad. He drove the steel faster and better than any other man. Most steel drivers used a ten-pound hammer. He used two twenty-pound hammers, one in each hand.

Clang! Clang! How he made those hammers ring! Hour after hour, he never missed a stroke. The shaker held his drill. The waterman threw water on his blazing hammers, so they wouldn't catch fire. John Henry's booming voice rang out up and down the line:

Ain't no hammer (Clang!)
In these mountains (Clang!)
Rings like mine, boys (Clang!)
Rings like mine. (Clang!)

Thanks to John Henry, the new railroad line moved right along. The tracks stretched through forests. They cut through hills and canyons. Then they came smack up against a monster: Big Bend Mountain.

Big Bend was too big to build around. The crew would have to drive their drills right through the middle. They would have to build a tunnel a mile and a quarter long. It would be the longest tunnel ever built.

A thousand men worked on the Big Bend Tunnel. They worked in smoke and dust, darkness and danger. And leading the way was the King of the Steel Drivers, John Henry.

21

One day, a city slicker showed up at camp. He was selling a new kind of drill, powered by steam. The salesman said, "This steam drill can drive steel faster than ten men put together."

The workers looked at the steam drill. They saw a metal monster bristling with tubes and knobs and dials. They saw a future when machines would rob men of their pay and their pride.

Then John Henry stepped forward. "Before I let a machine beat me, I'll die with my hammer in my hand."

So the contest was set. Who could drill faster: a machine or the world's best steel-driving man?

Folks came from miles around to watch the race. The captain blew his whistle. "Go!"

Whoosh! Clang! John Henry swung his mighty hammers.

Bang! Crash! The steam drill roared to life.

All morning long, John Henry's hammers rose and fell. His arms ached, and his insides felt like they were on fire. At lunchtime, he took a cool drink of water. Then he hammered away, faster and faster.

All that time, the steam drill pumped up and down. Men shoveled coal into its belly. They poured water into its boiler. Clouds of steam and dust and smoke billowed out from inside the mountain.

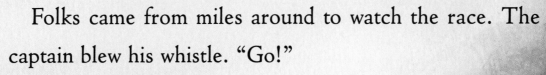

Finally, the sun went down, and the captain blew his whistle. The judges measured the holes. John Henry had drilled fourteen feet into the rock. The steam drill had only gone nine.

All the people cheered and shouted. John Henry just laid down his hammers. He sank to the ground. He closed his eyes with a smile. He had beat the machine, but his great heart had burst doing it.

They buried John Henry beside the Big Bend Tunnel. On a quiet night, you can still hear his hammers ringing. You might even hear a deep voice singing softly in the darkness:

Died with a hammer in my hand.
Here lies a steel-driving man.

ABOUT JOHN HENRY

Many people believe that the legend of John Henry is based on a real man. He may have been born a slave in the South before the Civil War. When the war ended, he went to work as a steel driver for the railroads.

The real John Henry might even have won a race with an early steam drill. The race probably didn't kill him, though. Like many other railroad workers, he may have died in an accident or from breathing deadly rock dust. His story lived on in the songs of southern railroad gangs. The King of the Steel Drivers became a hero of the working men whose strong arms and spirit helped America grow.

Our tale of John Henry is based mainly on stories retold by Harold W. Felton in JOHN HENRY AND HIS HAMMER (1950) and on stories and folk songs collected by Scott Reynolds Nelson for his book STEEL DRIVIN' MAN: JOHN HENRY, THE UNTOLD STORY OF AN AMERICAN LEGEND (2006).

WORDS TO KNOW

Civil War The war between the Northern and Southern states, fought from 1861 to 1865.

legend A story that has been passed down from earlier times. Legends may be based on real people and events, but they are not entirely true.

plantation A very large farm.

railroad ties Wooden beams that support the rails on a railway track.

shaker A railroad worker who held the drill for the steel driver and gave it a turn after each blow from the hammer.

steel drill A steel rod with a sharpened point. It looked like a very large nail.

steel driver A railroad worker who made holes in rock by hitting the steel drill with a heavy hammer.

timber Wood that is used for building.

TO FIND OUT MORE

BOOKS

Kessler, Brad. *John Henry: The Legendary Folk Hero*. Rowayton, CT: Rabbit Ears Books, 2000.

Krensky, Stephen. *John Henry*. Minneapolis, MN: Millbrook Press, 2007.

Ottolenghi, Carol. *John Henry*. Columbus, OH: McGraw-Hill Children's Publishing, 2004.

WEBSITES

American Folklore: John Henry
www.americanfolklore.net/folktales/wv2.html
Storyteller S. E. Schlosser tells the tale of John Henry's race against a steam drill.

National Public Radio: John Henry
www.npr.org/programs/morning/features/patc/johnhenry/#audio
Click on the links at the left of the webpage to listen to early recordings of the ballad of John Henry.

Voice of America's American Stories in Special English: John Henry
www.manythings.org/voa/stories/John_Henry.html
Read along as storyteller Shep O'Neal tells a tale of John Henry's adventures.

ABOUT THE AUTHOR

VIRGINIA SCHOMP has written more than seventy books for young readers on topics including dinosaurs, dolphins, American history, and ancient myths. She lives among the tall pines of New York's Catskill Mountain region. She enjoys hiking, gardening, watching old movies on TV and new anime online, and, of course, reading, reading, and reading.

ABOUT THE ILLUSTRATOR

JESS YEOMANS was born and raised on Long Island, New York, and grew up with a love of art and animals. She received her Illustration BFA at the Fashion Institute of Technology. She has been featured in many exhibits and has been awarded numerous awards and honors for her artwork.

Jess works as a freelance illustrator in Brooklyn. She enjoys drawing and painting, snowboarding, animals, cooking, and being outdoors. To see more of her work, visit www.jessyeomans.com.

Published in 2014 by Cavendish Square Publishing, LLC
303 Park Avenue South, Suite 1247, New York, NY 10010

Website: cavendishsq.com

This publication represents the opinions and views of the author based on his or her personal experience, knowledge, and research. The information in this book serves as a general guide only. The author and publisher have used their best efforts in preparing this book and disclaim liability rising directly or indirectly from the use and application of this book.

CPSIA Compliance Information: Batch #WS13CSQ

All websites were available and accurate when this book was sent to press.

LIBRARY OF CONGRESS CATALOGING-IN-PUBLICATION DATA
Schomp, Virginia.
John Henry, steel-driving man / retold by Virginia Schomp ; illustrated by Jessica Yeomans. — 1st ed.
p. cm. — (American legends and folktales)
Summary: Retells the life of the legendary steel driver of early railroad days who challenged the steam hammer to a steel-driving contest.
Includes bibliographical references.
ISBN 978-1-60870-441-5 (hardcover) ISBN 978-1-62712-016-6 (paperback) ISBN 978-1-60870-607-5 (ebook)
1. John Henry (Legendary character)—Legends. [1. John Henry (Legendary character)—Legends. 2. African Americans—Folklore. 3. Folklore—United States.] I. Yeomans, Jessica, ill. II. Title.
PZ8.1.S3535Joh 2012
398.2—dc22
[E]
2010023593

EDITOR: Deborah Grahame-Smith

ART DIRECTOR: Anahid Hamparian   SERIES DESIGNER: Kristen Branch

Printed in the United States of America